The King of Spain's Daughter

Christine Gray and Teresa Foster

Blackie Children's Books

I had a little nut tree,
    Nothing would it bear
But a silver nutmeg
And a golden pear;
The King of Spain's daughter
Came to visit me
And all for the sake
Of my little nut tree.

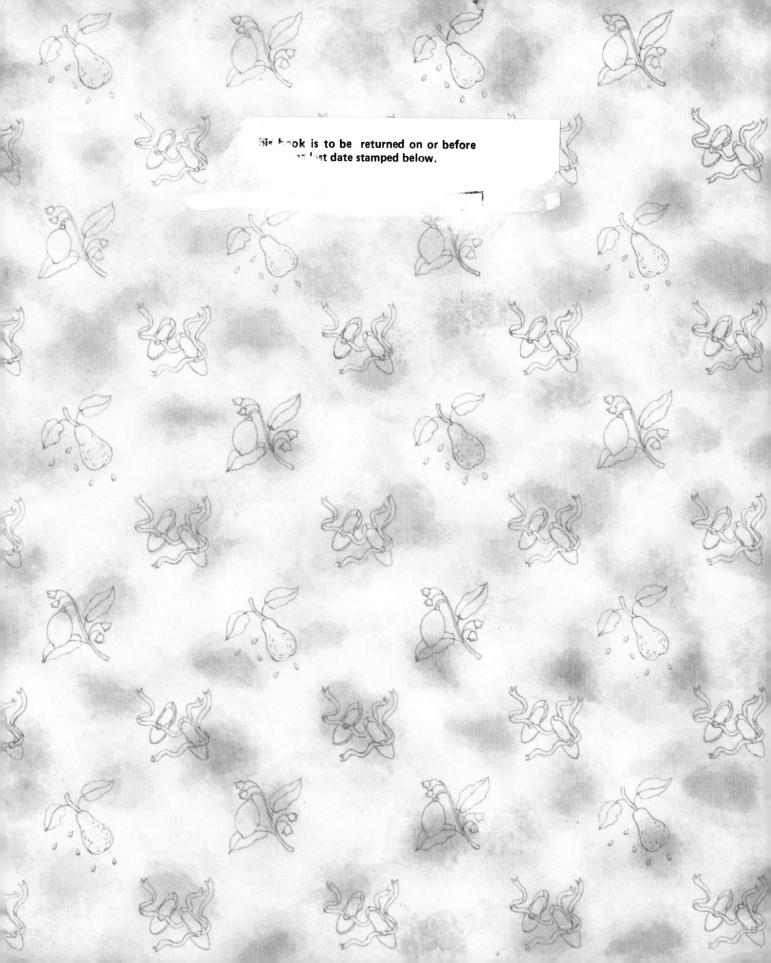

BLACKIE CHILDREN'S BOOKS

Published by the Penguin Group
Penguin Books Ltd. 27 Wrights Lane, London W8 5TZ England
Penguin Books USA Inc., 375 Hudson Street, New York, New York 10014, USA
Penguin Books Australia Ltd. Ringwood, Victoria, Australia
Penguin Books Canada Ltd. 10 Alcorn Avenue, Toronto, Ontario, Canada M4V 3B2
Penguin Books (NZ) Ltd. 182-190 Wairau Road, Auckland 10, New Zealand

Penguin Books Ltd. Registered Offices: Harmondsworth, Middlesex, England

First published 1993
1 3 5 7 9 10 8 6 4 2
First Edition

Text copyright © Christine Gray, 1993
Illustrations copyright © Teresa Foster, 1993

The moral right of the author and illustrator has been asserted

Printed in Hong Kong by Wing King Tong Co., Ltd.

A CIP catalogue record for this book is available from the British Library

ISBN 0216 93214 9

I opened the door to see that . . .

The King of Spain's daughter had come to visit me.

'So that's your old nut tree,' she said.

'Bet you can't climb as high as me.'

She couldn't wait to play hide and seek,

but she wasn't much good at hiding.

Next door had never seen anything like it.

'Is this your royal carriage?' she asked.

I told her not to go too fast,

but we couldn't keep up with her.

I let her play in my sandpit, but

'I wonder what this is?' she said.

My mum had to say sorry to Mr Glover.

I had to lend her my best jumper.

We were just having our tea, when . . .

her Dad came to fetch her.

Mum was going to tell him what had happened,

but she changed her mind.

He watched the football with my dad.
We had to look for her clothes.

She didn't say 'Thank you for having me'

but she left me a present.